No Swimming for Nelly

Valeri Gorbachev

Holiday House New York

Mommy gave Nelly a new swimsuit.
And Nelly looked marvelous.

She looked marvelous
from the front.

She looked marvelous
from the side.

From the other side.

And even from below.

"It's for swimming,"
said Mommy.

"No swimming for me," said Nelly.
"Why not?" Mommy asked.

"Because the water is cold . . .

"I don't like waves . . .

"I don't like water in my eyes and nose . . .

"and because water scares me!"

"I like my swimsuit.
But I don't like swimming."

So Nelly wore her swimsuit
while biking . . .

playing basketball . . .

having dinner at the fancy restaurant . . .

and while she was
sleeping.

One day, Mommy said to Nelly, "I have a surprise.
We're going to visit Grandma."
"Yay!" said Nelly. "I can show her my swimsuit!"

"Of course," Mommy said. "Grandma's going to teach you how to swim."

"No swimming for me," Nelly said.

Nelly and Mommy took
a short plane ride, and
Grandma met them at
the airport.

Soon they were at
Grandma's house . . .

where Nelly saw all of Grandma's trophies. Grandma was
a swimming champion!

"I see you're all ready for your first lesson," Grandma said.

"No swimming for me," Nelly said. "But can I watch you?"

Grandma and Nelly walked to the pool.

It was very big.

Then Nelly sat in a chair and watched Grandma dive into the water and race across the pool—five times without stopping! Grandma was still a champ.

"Come on in," Grandma said.

Nelly dipped a toe . . . then a foot . . . and then an ankle.
The water wasn't even cold.

Soon she was up to her waist in water. Nelly thought
she'd be scared. But she wasn't.

Grandma showed Nelly how to
blow bubbles. Nelly really liked the
bubbles she made.

Then Grandma showed Nelly how to float and kick and move her arms.

"Time for dinner!" Mommy called.
"But I want to keep swimming!" Nelly said.

At dinnertime, Nelly practiced blowing bubbles.

She practiced moving her arms and kicking too.

Nelly even practiced in
her sleep.

When Nelly went back to the pool the next day,
she swam like a champion.

Just like Grandma!